MEMORIES OF MONTSERRAT

by Dr. Irene S. Prospere

Order this book online at www.trafford.com
or email orders@trafford.com

Most Trafford titles are also available at major online book retailers.

Printed in Victoria, BC, Canada.

ISBN: 978-1-4269-1944-2 (sc)

*Our mission is to efficiently provide the world's finest, most comprehensive book publishing
service, enabling every author to experience success. To find out how to publish your book,
your way, and have it available worldwide, visit us online at www.trafford.com*

Trafford rev. 12/3/2009

 www.trafford.com

North America & international
toll-free: 1 888 232 4444 (USA & Canada)
phone: 250 383 6864 ♦ fax: 812 355 4082

Foreward

MY FELLOW Montserratians, as the years wane and I think of my home, I think of days past and the fun I had growing up with my siblings, cousins and friends. I think of the characters that used to live in my village, Collins Ghaut, a section in St. John's, Montserrat. I remember walking barefoot to and from school and getting up before the sun to do all my chores. I have fond memories of my beautiful mother and my father who loved to threaten people with his shot gun. Both have long since gone to be with the Lord and I rejoice in the way that they raised me. I remember the freedom that my brothers Wellington, Daniel, Stanley, Clyde, Everton and my sisters Mildred, Inez and Elizabeth (affectionately called Babylyn) had of going to one house or another in our village and being welcomed with open arms and a plate of food. There was my Aunt Ellen, Aunt Bertie, Aunt Molly, Aunt Daisy, Uncle John and my grandparents William & Frances Weekes and William & Caroline Allen and many others who treated all of us as their own children. My main purpose of putting pen to paper of all the memories, stories I heard, people I used to know and the many treasured friends, is for my future generations to someday read this book and to never forget that the most important things in life is not riches or fame but family. Though some of these stories may seem familiar to some who are reading this, some characters appearing in this work are fictitious and some names have been changed to protect the innocent. Any resemblance to real persons, living or dead, is purely coincidental.

Dr. Irene S. Prospere

Chapter 1
A BRIEF HISTORY

S o, to those of you who are not from Montserrat you may be asking, "what is it and where it is?' Montserrat is known as the Emerald Isle of the Caribbean. Montserrat is a tiny Caribbean Island situated between Antigua, Guadeloupe and Dominica. It is a British Colony but rich in Irish and African heritage. Montserrat was once hailed as the most beautiful Caribbean island with its lustrous green mountains and foliage, beautiful sandy beaches and a haven for tourists. The people are said to be the friendliest of all the Caribbean Islands, until it was spoiled by the sleeping volcano that began erupting in 1995.

In spite of or rather *"despite of"* as fellow Montserratians would say, we have survived and have started once more to thrive and show the world how resilient the people of Montserrat truly are. We must never let our culture and our heritage be overtaken and or overrun by others. There are many tales, stories, anecdotes and jokes about Montserrat and the people of Montserrat. Do not be fooled, the people of Montserrat are bright and well educated. We have produced Doctors, Lawyers, psychologists, social workers, a man who can be Governor and even Attorney General. I tip my hat to all of you.

Most Montserratians are Christians. They go to church every Sunday morning and they believe in taking care of their church and their parson, but they also like to tell jokes, tall tales and what we call "Jumbie stories". You would be surprised at some of the most intelligent people who believed that Jumbie *"me a stow"*, or that some of the tales were actually true... (*"me a stow"*) means that there were Ghosts and or Jumbies around. Some people said they saw them, some people said they heard them. You can believe what you want to believe and throw away the rest.

We are descendants of slaves and our culture is from Africa. We continue some of their customs and tradition which is where we get our folklore. I do not want the new generation and those to come to forget the best of Montserrat, our heritage, stories, songs and the way it used to be. Life was good even though we were not rich. Most people were able to live and survive off the land.

Montserratians are known to be one of the friendliest people in the world not just the Caribbean. Every morning your neighbors say *"good morning nybor"*, they do the same to strangers and visitors on the street. We are famous for our warm hospitality and polite greetings. *"Howdy nybor, good morning nybor, (Neighbor) God be with you"*. *"An how you a do dis morning neighbor?"* *"Tank de lord me wake up dis morning neighbor"*. In translation (for those who might have forgotten and those who don't know) *"good morning neighbor, and how you are this morning, God be with you and how are you doing this morning"*.

I consider myself one of the true born Montserratians. I am from a little place called Collin Ghaut. I love to be called a Collin Ghautian. My entire family, father, mother, grand parents and siblings along with a few other distinguished people, are all true 'Collin Ghuatians'.

I really love when I return and the immigration officers especially the ones that don't know me ask *"How long you staying ma'am?"* and I reply *"A yah me born."* *Where are you staying ma'am"?* *"Whey night catch me"* would be my whimsical retort. Sometimes I want to pull it with the new immigration officers but *"me fraid"* because I don't know if they would take insult because don't understand our Montserrat ways. To translate, *"I was born here and wherever night catches me that's where I will stay"*.

On those occasions that I go to Montserrat, I think I am in a foreign place with all the different faces and languages and those who are attempting to replace our culture with theirs. But like my grandmother would say *"Notten tall go so. Me nar ley uhm happen"*. In case you have forgotten (*Nothing go like that... I will not let it happen.*). I will continue to call Montserrat my home no matter where I roam up or down this world. I have already told my family my wishes, bury me in Montserrat or else. This book is about memories and recollections of growing up in Montserrat. So as a good friend of mine used to say *'wha fo u a fo u and wha no fo u lef um lone"*. In other words, believe what you will. Some of writings are in our colloquial dialect and I hope that you as the reader will enjoy it.

My special thanks to Dr John Stanley Weekes; Maude Meade; Leonora Weekes; Elsa Lee; Gwendolyn Rawlins; Margaret Lindsay; Everton Weekes; Patrick Sweeney; and Rose Piper for contributing some of their stories and memories and for just jogging my memory of things that I had forgotten.

Chapter 2
HOW IT USED TO BE

H AVE YOU ever wondered how our parents made it without jobs? How they were able to put food on the table and provide for their families? They worked hard. Some of our folks toiled from sun up to sun down in their fields to plant food for their families. That was a very good thing. We had all the food one could eat and some left over to give away and even sometimes to sell to make extra money.

Sometimes, no matter how small, there was a piece of relish in your food, and when no relish was available there was peas and long foot Cabbage or Spinach to replace the relish. We did not know at the time how nutritious those items of food were but don't be fooled, our fore parents knew exactly what was good for us. They knew the right foods to give us.

I remember all the bush tea they used to make us drink "*to tek the gas out a u stomach*". Our mothers and grandmothers had a different bush for every kind of ailment or if not, they send us down to the clinic for the Worm Oil to clean us out. Remember the worms that we used to pass? I think we should go back to the good old days when we had a good cleansing.

If you had a cold, you boil the Tezan, the trumpeter, and the Tobacco bush; the fever grass for a fever; information bush for inflammation; Ram goat bush for everything; sour sop bush and apple bush to move the gas; White head for belly ache; and Pump coolie to cool down your body and purge your blood;

If you had high blood pressure they knew what to boil; If you had pain in your chest they say *"you pip drop"* and of course their was always someone in the village, who knew how to pull up your pip with some concoction.

Nearly everybody drank their cup of bush tea first thing in the morning to take the gas out of their stomach including other things from the body. You would boil your tea and the sweet smelling aromas would tantalize your taste buds while you wait.

Yes, those were the good old days. This is how we lived back in the days before America and London called and people got sophisticated and forgot their roots. We would get up in the morning, did our work (what they now call chores,) and go to school on time. The morning was long because your parents woke you up really early to make sure everything is done before you go to school. When you get to school you better be on time and your hair combed, teeth, finger nails and foot clean or else here comes out the strap.

May all my children, grandchildren and generations to come read this book and through my memories and experiences appreciate Montserrat as it was in the good old days. I hope they appreciate that people survived by raising animals to kill, eat and or sell to make ends meet for their families; others planted cotton, and when the time came to sell cotton everyone who did so was rich. They had money to spend and spare. The children got new clothes and things were plentiful back then.

Yes, our parents were very resourceful knowing how to make ends meet and how to put nutritious meals together for their families. They were wise. There were good times and some bad times but through it all there were fun times for the children. I remember when we had no T.V. or even a radio to listen to so we played games, all kind of games such as …

Skipping, we had no skipping rope so we made our own by pulling a long string from the vine of the tree. We had better skip rope than what a stow now but it cost us nothing but our strength to pull it. No matter what pretty jump rope you have now, nothing could compare with our string. It used to be thick and heavy and sometimes all like twelve people used to be under the rope skipping.

We played hop scotch by marking boxes in the road. We used chuckle -rock and or gooseberry to play, they grew from the trees.

Marbles was a novelty but they came later.

We played cricket, and we made our own bats from coconut branches or some of the boys who were creative hew the bat out of Man Jack wood.

We played Rounders, what they call soft ball now. We used cherry seed to play games. We exchanged mangoes for cherry seed with the children from Drummonds, Rendezvous, Gerald's and Davy Hill. Yes, we learned early how to bargain with them for our goods. They had cherry, we had mangoes so we bartered twelve cherries for two mango. We played all kinds of games to keep us occupied and happy.

My Uncle John used to conduct organized games. Able cable noble man was his favorite game. *"Able cable noble man a man can do whatever he can, able cable noble man"*. Each person would pretend to be playing an instrument such as a guitar, mouth organ, fife, concertina, drums, banjo, etc. and when Uncle John played your instrument you had to play too or he would say *"Stop the band"* and everyone would say *"What for"* and he would call out the person who did not play their instrument on time and that person would get as many lashes he deemed fit and the game would start over.

Chapter 3
CELEBRATIONS

H ARVEST SUNDAYS were the big highlights for the people of Montserrat. People waited a whole year to bring the biggest and best of their crops to donate to their churches on Harvest Sunday. The Saturday before Harvest Day, the members showed up and cleaned the church from top to stall. People would then show up with their gifts. The church was decorated with Sugar Cane; Coconut; Dasheen; Yams; Cassava bread; Oven baked bread, flowers and coconut branches. All the women wore new clothes for harvest. You don't dare show up in any old clothes or something you wore before. Harvest was the highlight of your church life. If you did not have new clothes you stayed home. That was just the way it was. Beginning in late September, Harvest started at some of the smaller churches. The month of October the celebrations were a bit bigger. Churches used to be full as people from other churches and villages showed up for Harvest Sunday celebration.

The people from the villages cooked goat water, baked cakes and other goodies, because when church over, that's when the eating starts. Most people would go to either their family home, or if you happen to go to a celebration in another village you would always get invited to another church member's home to eat and drink. I remember as a child that my grandmother, Barber Weekes used to get up early and start cooking because as far as I know she had the most family I ever saw, coming from Long ground, Farms and Harris's. She would fuss and fuss and say, I have to cook and be ready for Gertrude children. Thank God they showed up most of the time. She would get to fussing. We had this joke going. I believe every body that came from the East was related to my grandmother or all they would have to say was "good afternoon Aunt Guppy" and a plate would be on the table in no time.

The two biggest harvests celebrations were held at St. George's church, which they use to call Harris's Harvest and the other was St. John's Harvest. Lots of people go to Harris's Harvest. But, the biggest by far which is also the last harvest of the year, was St John's Harvest. Let me tell you, St John's people knew how to plant food and save the best of their crops for St John's Harvest. I remember how beautifully the church was decorated. Foods of all kinds and variety were abundant. Sometimes, men used to climb the roof pole to put food in every nook and cranny of the church. No space or opening was safe from the decorators.

Who could ever forget the choir? The choir usually saved their best Anthem for Sunday. All the ladies young and old were dressed in their most opulent attire because in the afternoon was the Cantata.

The Cantata used to be like a talent show. Everyone practiced and were ready to show case their talent. There would be singing, playing of instruments, reciting of poetry or performances of whatever talent people had.

The next morning, bright and early, people came to sell the food. We as children used to hang around hoping they did not get all the sugar cane and bread sold because they would give the leftovers to us.

Starting in late October, it was time to start preparing for Christmas even before Harvest was over. Time to gather firewood to stack up for Christmas, especially if you were going to kill and roast a pig. The best firewood was Cusha wood or Cinnamon wood because it was believed that they burned the longest. Our elders believed in stocking up wood way before what was called 'busy week', because, *"nobody pick wood during Christmas time"*.

On the 5th of November we celebrated Guy Fawkes' night or Bon Fire Night. This celebration symbolized the foiling of a plot to blow up the House of Parliament and kill King James 1, in London back in 1605 by Guy Fawkes and some of his friends. We would light our flam bow and motor tires, anything that would give a good blaze. People who don't normally come out at night are out reveling. Bands would be playing music, masqueraders start practicing their dancing and people were in a festive mood.

We children used to call it Star Light Night, because the shops used to sell star light and the children used to buy them either single or in a pack. I remember that in order to get money to pay for our star light we used to collect bottles and sell them back to the shops especially to Mr. Hampsey because he had his Kola factory and needed bottles. This is the beginning of Christmas celebration as every night you either hear a band, masqueraders or serenaders also called carolers practicing.

The week before Christmas is always called 'busy week'. This is the time when the house is cleaned from top to bottom. All the furniture is put outside so that even the walls can be washed down. My mother used to take down the old curtains because it was time for new ones. People used to walk around the villages to see what kind of curtain others were putting up so they could go buy the same one. But sometimes they get fooled, my mother used to put up one from some years ago that she figured people won't remember and she would wait until Christmas eve to sew the new one and put it up and then, on Christmas morning, the house is bright and shining and looking brand new.

On the night of the 23rd, that's when they killed the pig. We used to go to sleep early so we could wake up when we hear the pig start squeeling. Sometimes, whoever killed the pig would start throwing something in the fire to roast and the smell would wake you up, if you were not up already.

It is a tradition to set the "Jumbie table" which is a table set for the spirits of our dead ancestors to come and feast on Christmas Eve. There would be dire consequences for anyone who interfered with the food before the spirits had come and gone. So, all day, people were cooking, from the pig head to the foot. The head and the foot were used to make Souse. Most of that went on the jumbie table because as they say *"e no taste too good when e fresh so e would taste better de next day"*.

The belly was used to make the pudden *(Pudding)* some of that go on the table too. You fry up the liver, cook some yellow yam, some dasheen, some sweet potato, some cassava bread, home made or special order bread, some cake, especially coconut tart, fry up Pork and ham and all these go on the table. Not one part of the pig is wasted. The table is not complete without some hard cheese and some raw salt fish and of course the drinks such as sorrel, coconut water, rum, wine, perks punch, Gin, Brandy and water.

I remember the serenades. I could not wait for them to come by our house to sing Christmas carols outside our door. We loved it when people who could really sing came by. The tradition was, between November and early December they already come by and sing a song leaving their names, such as Harris & Company or Daley & Company and the likes. So, on Christmas Eve night when they came we would already have their money prepared for them. Some people never serenade you before Christmas Eve, so when they come and sing you either don't open your door or you give them small change because you're keeping the real money for the Serenaders.

Christmas morning was my favorite time, everybody would get up early to see what they got for Christmas. There was no big Santa Claus stuff going on because we already knew who Santa clause was. For the girls there was a cloth doll sewed by your mother just a little bit different from the one last year. For the boys, there would either be marbles or a ball or a whistle and a flute on the head of a balloon, all of us received loads of balloons of all different colors. We were happy and contented with our gifts. We were so happy because we knew we are about to get the biggest gift of all the biggest breakfast of the year. They always make sure that they cook the Salt Fish that was on the Jumbie Table. They remove the souse and pudding from the table to warm up. Every child received a whole bread or Johnnie cake and Cassava bread and a big can/cup of cocoa or tea with milk. No bush tea on Christmas morning.

After breakfast, it was time to go to church or sometimes, we would go to church first. It all depended on the time of the church service. The rest of the morning was good times because for one day we had no work to do after the breakfast dishes were washed. We would play with our toys and stay inside because this is a quiet time just like Sundays.

After midday the celebrations really began. Masqueraders would be dancing, the string bands were playing and even steel bands would play if there was one. These revelers would go from house to house and performed, and you give them money or they eat food, they drink their sorrel or liquor and move on to the next house. When it was evening time, they would gather in the street and play and people just dance, eat, drink and make themselves merry.

If you ever missed out on Christmas day, it is something you never forgot. I remember that my brother, Everton, went singing out for the first time playing his guitar for Miss Fanny Bunksa and her group. They stayed out all night so Everton when he came home he went straight to sleep. I guess that there were so many of us in the house that we forgot all about him and when he woke up it was evening time, he had missed out on his Christmas day. He was really vexed.

There were some very good masquerades who could dance; Jim Galloway; Steamer, Brothers Gam, Dickey Bull, and Titus. Titus started dancing since he was a little kid so he was really good. But, the most memorable masquerader was the one they call John Bulla. John Bulla used to put a big stone on his chest, while lying backwards on his toes and fingers, and one of the other masquerades use to get a sledge hammer and break the stone on his chest. People use to flock around to see that and throw down plenty money. It was a tradition and it still is to throw down coins for the masqueraders and as fast as you throw the money down, they see it and rush for it.

The 26th of December is known as Boxing Day. This is a bittersweet celebration as it is a reminder of the misery of slavery. But for us we made it a chance for us to celebrate our freedom and how far we have come. People used to dress in their costumes; Miss May Barzey as the leader; Miss Dorris Harris; Miss Nelly O'Garro; Miss Fanny Bunksa, these were the leaders of guppies. They were dressed in their house coats or gowns with their best panties on and some other young girls following them in the band. The official Christmas time Band was Thomas Harris on the Horn; Fred white playing Yuke Banjo; John Fararee playing the Rhythm Guitar; Harry O'Garro on the Base Guitar; Jim Buntin on the Bomb Pipe; Georgie Sweeney on the Bomb Pipe; Brothers Fenton on Guitar; Sy Buntin playing the Horn; Gran Allen on the Shak Shak; Hammy Blake on the Shak/Grudge; and Tweed on the Bump Pipe. Their favorite song to for the Guppies to dance to goes something like this;

When you hear the music play show me you panty
When you hear the music play Show me you panty

The Guppies used to be grown women and young girls and they would dance around in circle then they would throw their gowns on top of their heads and show their pretty panties. Oh! how the crowd used to roar. Whomever had on the prettiest panty get the most money. Those were happy times, those were the good old days.

I have to tell you about my friend Miss Rosy Barzey, what a Reveler. Miss Rosy used to dress up in some costumes and play music with her concertina in her hand. The only thing was, Miss Rosy could not play her concertina and no one had the heart to tell her that she could not play. She would make a whole lot of noise with her concertina and she danced to her own music. Every day she dressed in a different costume with her concertina and she would just be dancing and playing up and down the street and she would make a lot of noise so that she had a large crowd following her.

On the 27th is St John's day. The party was in St John's. People from all over the Island head to the St John's day festivities. The older ladies used to get up to cook goat water to sell. There was also tub ice cream that was homemade. I remember how some people would charge a penny to turn the handle to let the ice cream churn that was good ice cream. There were games such as trying to throw the horse shoe over a bottle. I can't remember ever winning.

Things kind of cool off until New Year's day when everyone head to town. There were the street jump ups and Masqueraders from all over the island, guppy troops and parades every body reveling and happy.

People use to go from one house to the next sometimes just to have a drink or nimble on a piece of pork, cheese, or maybe even some food. They used to say *"good morning or good afternoon Gassup, compliments of the season to you"*, and out would come the bottle of whatever and some food on the table. Those were the days of comrade and friendship.

Chapter 4
LEGENDS AND FOLKLORE

T HERE ARE the Jumbie stories, tales of long ago and yes the jokes that are neither tales nor stories but just jokes and sometimes the strange behaviors of my fellow Montserratians. Please take what is written in the spirit that it is intended. Some things people make up and once they tell it on you it stick like 'bamit'. For those who don't know and are curious, what is bamit? Bamit comes from the sea. It will stick on you if it catches on to you in the seawater.

As Children, our grandparents, Aunts, uncles other relatives and yes our neighbors, were quite happy and content to tell us Jumbie stories and old wives' tales. To top it off when they were finished scarring you they blow out their lamps and expected you to go to sleep in the dark and get up in the dark to use the potty. You know what was the outcome, plenty children used to wet their beds.

Growing up in Montserrat we all heard the stories of the Jack O Lantern running after you; the Wedrigo singing when someone is going to die; the Loblolly Tree where the Jumbies lived; the Jumbie table on Christmas Eve; Jumbie come for your Child's name; Jumbie Dance; the Masqueraders dancing with the Mucko Jumbies; the Cattle

Horn that people burned in their coal pot and the Jumbies stay away and throwing some rum or other drink on the floor. It is tradition when you open a new bottle of liquor, or other drink for the Jumbie to throw some on the floor for them to drink.

The Jack O Lantern stories were rampant in days past. People used to see the big ball of fire from way off, and some would say *"before cat lick e ear it pan you"*. You had to hide in green bushes because if you hide under any kind of dry grass the Jack O Lantern would set you on fire. It depends on who you talk to. Some say they see a bird but others say they see fire.

The Wedrigo used to cry up and down the street and people say it is a big bird announcing when someone was going to die. You could hear the wings flapping. The old people would listen and understand what the bird was saying.

I grew up in the north so I can remember how early the shop keepers used to get up to start baking bread. Most mornings by 4 a .m. we had to be up. I was afraid of the dark because of all the jumbie stories that I was told. When it was my turn to get up early in the morning to help Aunt Kate bake bread, I use to make sure that I didn't walk in front or behind of anyone. I always walked in the middle. I figured, if the Jumbie was ahead, the person who was in front would get taken first and if the jumbie was behind, he would take the person in the back. Yes Sir, it was always the middle of the line for me.

I remember one such morning, as my parents and I stepped out of the gate and into the road we heard one big commotion up in the Lublaly tree by the grave yard that was in St John's Anglican Church. I started shaking in my boots. I was so scared that I started to scream. Aunt Kate (that is what everyone called my mother) yelled at me to shut my mouth and follow her. My father, Allen James never said a word. But, when I looked on his face I realized that he was just as scared as I was. We all rushed up the street and ran into the shop and locked the door. Even with the door closed, we could still hear that awful noise coming from the street. My father just kept saying to himself "ge me de shovel dig de grave, give me de shovel dig de grave". My father then said "not one but two".

The next morning the church bell started tolling not once but twice... one two three for man; one, two, three, four, five, for woman, Mass Ted and Miss Maggie Fly had died in the night. Believe what you want, but I think that the awful sound was the jumbie coming to take their souls so I quess the wedrigo was right.

My paternal grandmother, Caroline Caro Allen, affectionately known as Narna, regaled us with stories of Iron Case, Her words in Dialect: *"No body can pass Iron Case with fry fish unless you put dung a piece of de fry fish for de Jumbie dem will actually hole you up and kip you dey until dey get a piece".* One time Narna say; *" me me pan me way to Harris wid a tray of fry fish. Me modo no me tell me fo left piece, so me me a go pan me merry way, when somebody whole on pan de tray an me pull and pull and the sudden nar move an den me remembo how you supposed to lef sudden pan you way so me tek de tray off u me head, and put dung a piece of fish and den me no no wha happen but the pan get free and me run an run an go pan me way".*

Let me now explain that in English for those who cannot understand the Montserrat dialect. There was a village in Montserrat called Harris village. People from the North, had plenty of fish as we lived near to the sea, which was mostly calm. They would fry fish and send to the East, Trants, Farms, Harris, Bethel and Long ground. If and when you pass through this place called Iron Case, you had to put down a piece of the fish. As the story goes, Jumbie would hold on to the fish pan and keep pulling you back until you leave a piece for them.

All the St John's School children remember well the story of the diamond snake down in Pump Ghaut. "If you see the snake you get the comb from his head run to the sea and make sure that you beat the snake there of course, dip the comb three times and it will turn to Gold". Children really believe anything.

There was also the Mermaid in Pump Ghaut. Many stories have been told of people seeing the mermaid bathing its skin early in the morning and late in the evening.

There were rumors all the time that certain gentlemen from the North dealt with the devil. School children say that they heard the devil on his horse trotting up and down St John's Road or coming down Barzey River. As the story goes, there was a man from Quashy Spring who owed the devil so he decided to build a house in St. John's thinking that the devil would not find him. While his wife and children were sleeping, the devil came trotting though the house asking for the man, I guess you can't hide from the devil.

Chapter 5

THE STORIES

I BELIEVE THAT most children and some adults were afraid of the dark. I am one of those children who was very afraid of the dark. On one such night I can remember it vividly, we all were sitting on the steps in the bright moon light telling jumbie stories trying to scare each other. My mother got up and said that she was going to the store because she forgot something. A short while later, my brother Stanley went in the house. After a little while, Stanley came back out and he waited a little while and then told me to go into the house to light the lamp. As I was afraid of the dark I did not want to go so Stanley threatened to beat me with his belt if I didn't get into the house and light the lamp. I knew that the matches were over my mother's bed so I figured I could just close my eyes and go into her room to get the matches. I went into her room and stretched over her bed to take up the matches and as I opened my eyes and looked down their was a dead woman lying on the bed with her jaw tied up (that's is how they used to keep the bodies after someone dies in those days), and I screamed and screamed and I heard the dead woman laugh and somehow in the recesses of my mind I knew it was my mother and that's all I remember until I come to (I guess I fainted). What a fright those people gave me. If my mother did not laugh I do not believe that I would have woken up. Stanley and my mother had planned the whole thing to scare me. Those two could have killed me with fright. After that, you could not get me to go from one room of the house to the next after dark.

It was worst when I had to go and sleep at the home of my paternal grandmother. My Grandmother, Caroline Davis Allen called Narna Carro, was a character in herself. She had a masquerade whip not only to whip us but to drive the Jumbies and Ghosts away. She took pleasure in telling us all the jumbie stories and all the people who put Portuguese jumbie on her and you either had to agree with her or else she might just get mad and send you home in the middle of the night in the pitch blackness.

Imagine a very dark night. The lamp is out to save the oil, and you must go to sleep in the dark and the last thing you were told before you went to bed is how some jumbie is going to get you in your sleep. Your imagination would naturally run wild and you think that the jumbie is right there in the house. What do you think is going to happen when you go to sleep? More than likely, you will wet the bed. In my parents' house if anyone wets the bed the next morning your parents put you under the cold pipe as punishment for wetting the bed. Maybe if they were not telling all those Jumbie stories right before bedtime then we would have gotten up to go use the potty which was outside. You would have to go outside in the dark to use the potty.

At my house, there was a roll out cloth made from the flour bag and stuffed with Banana bush that my mother made by hand for all of us children to sleep on. Boys and Girls, if you wake up in the morning and your space is wet, you are going under the cold tap water. I use to make sure that my space was dry. I used to climb over to Mildred's space and every morning it was poor Mildred under the cold water. Mildred and Stanley suspected that it was me, so, one night, they switched places and I did not know. So I did my nightly ritual of crawling over to Mildred's side of the bed and started doing my business. Stanley grabbed me and called for Aunt Kate. Do you know that they did not wait until morning? They took me to the cold shower right then in the middle of the night, I could have caught a cold. I don't think I ever wet the bed again. I was more afraid of a cold shower than I was of the jumbie.

There was a woman in our village who died and the night after the funeral, one of my beloved teachers and her cousin were walking home from out Miss Daughter shop, when they reached the gate of the woman who died, there she was standing dressed in her white burial dress. They couldn't believe it, this was the woman who was just buried a couple of hours ago. They just looked at her and started running and by the time they reached their grandmother's house, she was up waiting for them because the woman came to her in a dream and told her that her two grand-daughters were staring in her face. She told their grand-mother that the only reason she did not do anything to them was because they were old friends.

A certain young man who had heard the story of what happened to my teacher and her cousin was walking home late one night. He heard walking coming towards him and all he could see was feet with two white sneakers. He moved to one side of the road and the two feet with white sneakers moved to the same side of the road with him so in his mind he swore it was a Jumbie following him so he ran into Miss Marly's house (remember that Ms. Marly had been bur-ied a couple of days before), the boy was so frightened he was sure Ms. Marley was following him. The next thing he knew he bumped into something, and he was scared out of his wits, it turned out to be this gentleman named Wheezy who was going the same direction as him all along. You see what can happens when your mind plays tricks on you.

There was this woman who had three friends, just before she died, she received a package from foreign and she shared the vest and panties between them. It is said that she came back from the grave to get her gifts back from the three friends. The first one she went to told her that she better go back where she came from because she never asked for the gifts. Shortly after that the woman had a stroke and it was bye bye for her.

The second woman bought a long chain and put it on her dog so that it could guard her house. The dead woman came to someone in a dream and told her that she was just waiting for the right time to strike. So, a few days later when the dog fell asleep the dead woman came through the window slapped her friend and in the morning when the family wake up, the woman had had a stroke and she was gone too.

But, woman number three was not scarred of no dead woman because she herself was a very powerful obeah woman. So, when the dead woman came for her she just burn her cattle horn and said incantations and the dead woman could not touch her. I remember when that story was going around that St. John's street was empty at dark. Every man, woman and child made sure that they were inside their houses before dark. People say the cattle horn is not only a musical instrument, when you burn it in the fire, it could run Jumbie.

Every Saturday, Narna Caro used to send us to wherever they killed the cattle to get her cattle horn. Sometimes we were lucky if Tanny Matthew don't beat us. But they used to share things because they were friends. Imagine Tanny was the mother Mercy following the Pastor everywhere. You know how the Mother Mercy was supposed to be holy and righteous, so Tanny never want any body to know she burned cattle horn.

One Saturday, Tanny went to town and she did not tell Narna Carro that she was going to town, so Narna was vex.

She took her Cattle horn and she a burned it. So, when Tanny come out by the gate and called out to Narna Carro to see if she had any goodies for her, Narna lied and say no (remember she was still upset that Tanny went to town without her, going to town was a big deal in those days), Tanny did not bother to come in because according to Narna she received her England money. (Narna felt that she did not want to share her money with her so that is why Tanny went to town without her). After Tanny left, a big black cat came to Narna's gate and started crying. Narna took out her masquerade whip and started cracking and dancing, She turned her behind to the south, she throw her dress on her head and was dancing and singing 'Turn back to narod turn, turn back turn back turn back". The cat got up and ran for his life (I think the cat was just scarred of seeing this woman looking crazy dancing around the yard. Narna thought that Tanny had sent the cat to get her soul).

There was an old man from Drummonds who used to ride his donkey everywhere. There was this girl who used to stone him and would poke a stick into the donkey so it would kick up and take off with the little old man. He used to get angry and complain to the girl's parents but the little girl continued to torment him anyway. The man used to say, "one day I will blind you". The old man died and shortly after that the girl became blind. She remains blind to this day.

Chaper 6
THE JOKES

THERE WAS a man from Underwood Mountain they called Junky Joe, every Sunday morning, he came to St John's Anglican Church and would bring a roast dumpling in his Jacket pocket so he could eat on his way home. One Sunday, Junky Joe fell asleep in church. When he woke up, the congregation was singing "Holy, Holy Holy" Junky Joe grab his jacket pocket and jumped up in church and shouted out, *'hold who, hold who, hold me fo tek way me dumpling'*.

The Pastor was in the pulpit preaching one day and he said everyone needs to take the enemy out of his bosom. One man pulled out a flat of rum and said *'see yum ya parson a dis you want'* (see it here Pastor, is this what you are looking for).

There was once a nice English pastor that was well liked by the people at first. But, after they realized that he was sent from England to come to 'straighten out the church' the parishioners did not like him anymore and started to give him a hard time especially the vestry members (these were supposed to be the people who helped him most). A young man who was well known by the villagers as a character or what one would call a jokester said to the pastor one day *"Pastor, I hear that the people and especially the vestry are giving you one hard time, but, I know for a fact that one of them is having an affair and he is a married man"*. The pastor said to him, *"is that true"* and he replied *"of course"*. The Pastor told him that he was going to give him some nice clothes so that on the next Sunday he can come to church and address the congregation and tell them what he knows. Sunday morning arrived and the man made sure he drank his rum and dressed in his nice new suit and went to church. The Pastor got up in the pulpit and said, *"We have a new member here today and he has something he wants to share with the congregation, this is a truthful man and you all must believe him"*. The man got up and walked to the pulpit and in a loud voice he said, *"as I was passing Parsons gate, I saw him kissing his servant Kate"*. The Pastor jumped up and said *"get out of my church you lying......* (just use your imagination).

There was a certain Pastor who could not read, but he liked to drink his rum. Usually, when he showed up to preach, he was drunk. The Sexton used to read the scripture for him so he could preach. One day when the Sexton was reading, the Pastor said to him *"Move your hand so that I could see what you are reading"*. The Pastor told the sexton to continued reading. The Pastor interrupted the Sexton again and said to him *"What did the Lord say"*, the Sexton with a straight face turned the page in the bible and said to the Pastor *"He says you will never get another drink of rum, until you pay up what you owe him"*.

There was this man, I will call no names, who was stoning a mango. He threw stone after stone and the mango would not drop. He climbed the tree, felt the mango and said to the mango *"okay, you think you bad, me a go show you who bad'"*. The man went back down to the ground and started stoning the mango again.

The same man was asked to count the pigs in the pen to see how many sow the pig had. He turned to Mass Jim and said *"Mass Jim, me count nine o dem but dis one ya a run around and me can't count e"*. (Mr. Jim, I counted nine but this one is running around and I can't count him).

There was a woman we called Miss Nan. A nice lady but you could not please her. Miss Nan used to have big needles and one day when I was making a Basket and my needle broke I asked Miss Nan to lend me her needle. As soon as I put the needle in the basket it broke. I knew I was in trouble. I went up to Mr. Howe shop and Ms Cashie helped me get a needle that was the same size and we rubbed it and did everything that we could to make it look old. I gave the needle to a friend to take to Miss Nan. The next thing I know the village was in an uproar because Miss Nan was screaming that I stole her needle and gave her a new one.

My friends Margaret and Polina used to come down by my house to catch water. One morning they said good morning to Miss Nan and she said to them *"if a you hafo grumble,no talk to me"*. The next morning they said a little louder, *"Good morning Miss Nan"* and she said *"if a you hafo shout pan me, no botha tell me notttin"* (if you have to shout at me don't bother tell me anything"). The next morning they just passed her bye and said nothing. This got her so mad that she went up to their grandmother's house to complain *"Miss Marma dem two women you have up ya a pass me an nar say nottin"* (the two women you have up here are passing me and not saying anything to me)".

You know back in the days on Sunday afternoons the young girls used to get dressed and go for a walk. Ms. Nan would turn to whomever was around and say *"look pan dem, they gone man hunting"*.

One morning Lenora, Inez and I were in the yard washing clothes and we heard screaming coming from the Miss Nan's house *"murder, murder, John Weekes a kill me"*. We ran to her house and Miss Nan had my Uncle John down on the ground with her hand around his throat choking the life out of him. It took the three of us to pry Miss Nan's hand from Uncle John's throat. We all just looked at each other because she was the one choking Uncle John but she was crying murder.

Growing up, there was this guy they called 'small eyes', they also use to call him 'Micey'. Well he used to live with Miss Nan. Miss Nan used go to mountain and come home late, so he would beg food from whomever he could. Whenever Miss Nan cook she put a plate of food in front of Micey, the plate was so high you couldn't see over on the other side. Micey used to put his head down and eat and then he would stretch and stretch all the while ignoring whomever would be standing around waiting to be paid back for the food he borrowed. Whenever anyone would ask back for the food that they gave him, he would just look at them as if they were crazy.

In 1962, when my brother Wellington come from England he brought home a record player. That was a novelty in those days as every body mostly had a gramophone. Those were the ones you had to whine up to make them work. Anyway, after he left to go back to England all the village children used to gather to hear the sweet reggae music. One day school was out so we played music all day, Miss Nan came by the gate and said *"Irene you no tink that man tired now, you have him a talk all day and if e no stop talk me a go up a de shop and tell Miss Kate pan you."*

On Sundays when we go to church no matter what happened you could not laugh as long as Miss Nan was sitting in her bench. Say for instance the pastor said something funny and you laughed and she happens to see you, if you see her get up when the church started singing the last hymn and she leaves before services is over, you knew you were in trouble when you went home because she just assumed you were laughing at her.

Do you remember as children how sometimes we can be very mischievous? One Sunday we decided we were going to take a handkerchief and make a brazier (what is known as a bra). All the girls sitting on the bench made a brazier and then we passed it back to the boys and they started making one. There was this boy we called Crazy Roy, when he made his brazier he placed it on his chest and of course we all laughed. Unfortunately for all of us children from Collins Ghaut, Miss Nan decided that we were laughing at her and did you know we all got a beating when we got home.

There was another lady who used to listen to her Radio, mostly the gospel station out of St Marten, Radio P. JD2. Most times the station she was listening to was some preacher begging for money and asking people to send in an offering. The poor lady thinking of herself as a good Christian, started putting the offering in the radio, one day, the radio stopped playing. She asked her grandson to help her figure out why the radio was not working and sure enough, when he opened the radio, it was full of money that is why it stopped working.

Another time as she was cooking her dinner and listening to her radio, she felt sorry for the man who was talking, she said to no one in particular *"that poor man me a talk all day and he must be hungry"*. So, she put a plate of rice in front of the radio for the man to eat.

I don't know about you, but I was afraid of masqueraders, Guppy, mucko Jumbie. Name it and I was afraid of it. Especially when people got dressed up to dance when it was Christmas time. They were all dressed in their scary costumes and I used to run from them. One Boxing Day morning, my mother sent me to the shop. When I approached the head of the road, I saw a masquerader coming, I ran into my Aunt Daisy's house and hid under the bed to get away from the masquerader. The masquerader followed me into the house and pulled me from under the bed and I started sreaming. It turned out to be Brothers Garne who was married to my cousin Joyce and this was their house.

This old lady had cooked herself some delicious flour porridge, she covered it and went into her garden. When she was ready to eat she came for her porridge but the pot was empty. She asked her grandson what happened to the porridge. The boy said *"granny me me a call you fo tell you dat when me cum home me see one big Portugese Ram cat in the pot drinking all de porridge".* The old woman was mad thinking that she made her porridge and the cat ate it but, if she had looked at her grandson's belly she would have realized who the 'Portuguese ram cat' was.

I remember this man they used to call Al Cox. Al used to go to Mountain everyday. One day he caught a big old rat. He said to the rat, *"if you want me to let you go, you have to tell me who is the greatest cricketer on earth".* The rat made a squeak and Al swore that he heard the rat say 'Weekes' and he replied to the rat *"you right man Weekes is the greatest cricketer on earth".* He swore that the rat was referring to Everton Weekes.

There was a man named John. S. Weekes from lower St. John's who gave some of the sweetest jokes.   He said one night he was sewing and things was so bad financially that he refused to light his lamp to waste oil. He said he was trying to thread his needle and he could not get it thread. He decided after awhile that he better light the lamp after all. To his astonishment it was a girl he had in his hand thinking it was a thread. This girl was a very thin girl so John S was trying to thread her into his needle.

Years ago, there was a sign on the St. Johns' Anglican Church that read. "No Cross no Crown". One morning to every one's astonishment, somebody removed the C from Cross and the C from Crown and left " No ross no rown."

There was this man who used to go visiting from house to house and no matter how often you ask him if he was hungry he said no. One night somebody followed him home to see what he was eating. It was porridge that he made, a rat had fallen in his porridge, he licked off the rat, and said , *"clean you come, clean you shall go"*.

As children, we all had names for adults that we said behind their backs amongst ourselves. We all called our Uncle John, 'John Bagger' but never to his face. But, my cousin Alwyn and my Uncle John had a battle going and Alwyn liked to annoy him so every time Alwyn saw him, he would say *"good morning John Bagger"* and my Uncle would be upset, he hated that name and Alwyn new it. So one day he went down to my Aunt Molly house and called out. *'Oh Molly Daley, warn your son Alwyn not to call me any John Bagger, if he can't call me Uncle John or Mass John, tell him no call me o tall"*. You can imagine the trouble that Alwyn got into with his mother.

One night at church during the service the Pastor called on this lady to read a scripture from Revelation 1:10. The scripture goes like this. "I am alpha and Omega, the first and the last". Unfortunately, this lady could not read, she had heard the scripture so many times and she got up opened the bible and said *"I am alcholado and Joemeger, the fuss and de last. Amen"*.

Most weddings used to take place on Wednesdays and after the wedding, the dancing start. Sometimes it's a regular dance but sometimes is the Jumbie dance. It went something like this. The family either kill a bull or a few sheep and goat and always roasted a pig. Because that is the real food for the jumbie. There was always rice, plenty of breadfruit and Dasheen and fungi. People come and eat and have a very nice time because there was also a lot of alcohol. If you were privileged enough to eat inside, the success of the party is measured by how many rounds they serve. Most weddings were held at Barba Weekes house, because she had the biggest dining room and table out a north, and she also had the biggest Iron Pot. When you cook the stew in that pot it was said to be the best and could feed a nation. Every one is merry until sun down, then they start cooking

the 'musicians dinner'.   They cook all the goat head and
foot and belly with whatever other meat was left over and
cover it down to serve later. Lord that food use to sweet man.
The musicians were a bunch of characters in they own right.
Here are a few of their songs that I can remember.

> When you wake a morning
> Tell you neighbor morning
> Morning neighbor morning
> Morning neighbor morning.
>
> Old man lek buddy tarm
> A way he a do wid young gal
> Old man lek Buddy tarm
> A wha he a do with young gal.
>
> Irene Good night, Irene Good night
> Good night Irene, Good night Irene
> I saw you in my dream.
>
> Matthew Johnny and he ain't do nothing
> Pam pa lam
> And he get six months for his young granddaughter
> Pam pa lam.
>
> Give it, If have it
> Give it with a willing mind
> What the Lord give to you
> Be it generous and true
> Give it with a willing mind.
>
> A little more oil in the lamp keep it Burning
> A little more oil in the lamp I pray
> A little more oil in the lamp keep it burning
> Keep it burning till the break of day.

Bam chikalay the chigger foot maya
Me grandmother me send me for water
She tell me lay me no trouble nobody
Damn neager man come feel up me la la.

Bam chicka lay the chigar foot mya
Bam chicka lay the chigger foot mya.

When I die, don't bury me a tall
Pickle my bones with alcohol
A bottle of rum at my head and my feet
And tell all the young girls that me die for rum.

Farm Bay Farm Bay
Farm Bay a wan bad bay
Come ley a we go day a farm bay
Farm Bay Farm By
Farm Bay a wan bad bay
A Farm bay kill me Marmy.
Farm Bay a one bad bay

The one and two polka.

Here are all the characters that Played in the Band for the Jumbie dance. They also played for weddings and parties.

Thomas O" Bart	On the Concertina
Largo	On the Concertina
Jackie Pepper	On the fife
Samuel Begna	On the fife
Charlie Buffonge	On the fife
Dicky Breel	On the Kittle drum
Pan Bag	On the Boom Boom Drum
Thomas Harris	On the Horn
Constable (Dada)	On the triangle
Harry Andy	On the Shack Shack

Marma Yarm   Wu Wu Drum
Jebb   Smaller Wu Wu Drum

The music was always sweet. The women would gather in their wide fluffy skirts and they dancing swing to the music with they partner, The musicians played, eat and drink and they started to get giddy. They would then call for the cadrills. The women would dance and throw their skirts on top of their heads as their partners twirled them around.

There was a certain woman from St John', no name, and she was the master turner. No sooner the call for Cordrills, she would throw her dress on her head and she would go into a trance and sometimes she would dance right out of the front door. She always see some spirit or if she is dancing because jumbie is on somebody, she always know where to go in the yard and dig up whatever people supposedly bury there.

When all the turning and dancing was over and you meet the same lady in the street she is as quiet as a lamb.

Chapter 7
CHARACTERS

ARRY USED to tell the story of how he became an Obeah Man. One day he was down on his luck, he had no money to buy food to feed himself or his poor mother so he went into town to try to get a day job. He said he tried to find something all day but he had no luck. He was waiting for a ride to go back to the country so he sat under M.S Osborne and this lady sat down next to him. She told him that she had a job for him. It seems that her child was going to secondary school and he was very smart and somebody was jealous of him and was trying to mess him up so they put something on him. When Harry showed up to her house in Corkhill, he saw a young man in the bedroom lying on his bed. He said the boy had a swollen jaw. He checked and realized that the boy had an abcess. He told the lady he wanted $500.00 to do the job, because it's going to be a big job. He walked from the house down to Isle Bay, where he caught a lizard, got some sand and he found some hair outside somebody house on his way back. When it was pretty dark, he told the woman to give him a basin and to leave the bedroom. He put out the light, poured the sand, hair and lizard in the basin. He then hit the boy one slap in his face and the abscess burst. He held the basin to the boy's face so that he could spit out everything into the basin. He carried out the basin to the woman and said, "*This is what they put in your son'*. The poor woman believed and hand over the money.

There was this lady who had twins and one died. The other one did not speak as he was growing up so everyone thought that he was mute. The woman decided that she needed an obeah to work on her child to get him to talk. So, she called on Harry Pen Rice. Harry got a coal pot and light it and together with his assistant Bapsey, they lifted up the boy and held him over the fire. When the heat got too the boy he said, *'the fire hot'*". I guess he could speak after all.

Miss Alice Dick told her husband Pappy Dick that she could not sleep at night because a Jumbie was on top of the roof of the house. Of course Pappy Dick called his number one obeah man, Harry. Harry went to the house and spent one night in Miss Alice's bedroom and told them the next morning that it was a really bad jumbie. He asked them to sleep somewhere else the following night so he could take care of the problem. During the night Harry cut down the breadfruit limb that was touching the roof of the house. They swore Harry was the best Obeah man they know.

There was yet another Lady who was not feeling well, so she called Harry and say she believe that there is jumbie in her stomach. So they called on Harry to come and get the jumbie out. Harry went to Ms. Peters store and bought two ounces of Peppermint drops. When he was getting close to the woman house, he started shaking up the bottle so the peppermint was frothing. He told the woma, close your eyes and drink this. The woman drank and she started passing gas. Every time the woman passed gas, Harry would count; Jumbie one, Jumbie two, Jumbie three, till he got to twelve. He said to the woman "*madam dem a de twelve baddest jumbies me ever came across*". The woman paid him handsomely.

Harry was walking in Plymouth one day and when he got to George Street, he pulled off his belt and was about to pull his pants down. When he got everyone's attention, he said, *"Father Moses make this law that man should shit to ease his maw. Woman, Woman, what a blessing, that you could shit without undressing*

But we unfortunate sons of man, could not shit without dropping our breaches", he proceeded to drop his pants in the middle of the street, two Police men came upon the scene and drag Harry off to Jail.

Pappy Dick went to town to sell his cotton and low and behold he realized that two bags were missing. He accused a man from Corkhill of stealing his cotton. So, he called his friend Harry Pen Rice and told him that he wanted the man dead. Harry took the money and went to Antigua go do his Job. Harry was a very boasting man, so with all that money in his hand he showed up at Police headquarters in Antigua and went to the canteen buying drinks for everyone and playing a big shot. After all the money was gone, and he hadn't killed anybody yet, Harry was wondering what to do next because he could not go back to Montserrat. Harry went to the canteen at the police headquarters to see if anybody would buy him a drink, but as it so happened, he was in the right place at the right time, he overheard that there was a bad accident in Montserrat and that they were going to fly the gentleman over to Antigua. As luck would have it for Harry, it turned out to be the same man that he was supposed to kill with his obeah. Unfortunately for the gentleman, he passed away in the night so Harry got on the next plane to Montserrat and went to see Pappy Dick to relay the good news. The Job was done. So much for Obeah.

I remember Parpa Weekes and his Big Big Mango tree. It was the only one in Montserrat so he used to cherish his tree and he never wanted anyone to pick his mangoes. So he use sit under the tree when he think school getting out waiting to see if they coming to pick his mango. But as soon as he get under the tree he fall asleep. So the children used to come and climb quietly over him and when he wake mangoes gone and he no see nobody.

I hear that people used to thief Parpa's coconut up Cat Ghaut. So Harry came to him and told him *"if you pay me a certain sum of money I will let you catch the man who stealing your coconut; when he get up in the tree, I will make sure he stick up there and can't get down".* Harry tricked one of his friends into going to steal the coconut and he told Parpa the exact time to go to check on his coconuts and sure enough, the man was up in the tree stealing the coconut.

There was another family and all the children were sick most of them had pain in their bones and they swore that somebody put a curse on the whole family. So they set up a Jumbie dance and asked this woman to come and do a jumbie dance for them so they could see what was happening. The woman told them she needed to come and case out the place the night before without any interference. So she went the night before and set up whatever she wanted under the door treacle. So the night of the jumbie dance when the musica started to play she started to dance and turn. She danced, threw her dress on her head and ask for the number one and two polka. She danced until she get outside. Then she said *"Dig up the door treacle".* Underneath there were all kinds of things that was supposed left there by the Jumbies. The family needed help to remove all the obeah stuff that they found.

Somebody say that there was a woman who was cooking soup at night and a centipede dropped in her soup while she was cooking. She tried to use her pot ladel get it out but she couldn't get it so she decided to leave it alone. When she shared her soup one of her young daughters ended up with the centipede brain in her food and she thought it came from a fish head. She said to her Mama *"me no me no you cook fish".* The mother said *"gal just eat what you get and ask no question".*

They say it was Christmas time and masqueraders were out serenading, so they came down to a certain house. They had a high window at the low side of the house and a little girl was trying to see the masquerades but her chin could only reach the window sill.   They say all of a sudden a jumbie picked her up and threw her outside. She fell on her chin and her chin twisted right out of place and turned her face around. There was a woman dancing guppy with the group and she went in a trance. She picked up the child and started dancing with her. She said " *lord this child interfered with the jumbie table*". She held the little girl's chin and pulled it back in place.   According to her the jumbie was only frightening the child so she don't touch no more jumbie table.

You know in the old time days people used to put spell on each other. Well the story goes, that this man stole this woman's money, so she me put a spell on him. This man was a fisherman and one day he went fishing. He saw a turtle and he went after the turtle. People say the turtle was beckoning him. He did not catch the turtle that day, so he decided to go back the next day. The next day, when they went fishing in the same area, there was the turtle. He told the other people in the boat that this time he was not coming back without the turtle. They say the turtle started beckoning him again and he followed the turtle. He went in the water after the turtle, and he never come back up.

You know how people could get names and the names stick on you. There was a woman who had five sons. She named them Sam Chunky, Wheezy, Parpa, Shitman and Tunko. Anyway, all the men bought a hand radio about the same time. Some of them bought boom boxes because they were loud and so they went up and down the road with their radio in their hand listening to calypso. There was a popular song called "Come ley a we go sukie come ley a we go". It was the most popular song in town. One day somebody was passing by and their radio was playing the song. Shitman decided to turn on his radio but the song was not playing something else was on. Shitman got mad and threw down his radio and said *"somebody thief the sukie out of me radio and me no want um no more".* He did not know that his radio was on a different station.

There was a certain man called Umbrey Weekes who only had two prayers that he repeated, one on Sunday and the other on New Year's day, on Sundays he would say *"Lord please to help me buy one bread when Sunday morning come, and please to keep me from the church yard"* (he was afraid of dying). Umbrey also used to make it a point of duty to pray this prayer every New Years morning, *"Lord thank you for letting me see another New Year's morning and help to live to see another Harvest Sunday".*

I remember two brothers called Sam and Mackey. Sam used to say *"Lord, me a ask you to please help me get to America, because as soon as me reach me a throw me-self under the first bus and let me mother and me father get the money".* (His mother and father were already dead.)

Mackey stole Ms. Brand's breadfruit and they took him to court. Now Mackey's legal name is Daniel Barzey. The Bailiff calls out, *'Daniel Barzey, Daniel Barzey'.* He said, *"coming my worship, guilty of ten breadfruit".* He did not wait to be sworn in or questioned he just plead guilty. The Magistrate asked him, *"Do you know lie from truth".* He said, *"yes sir, lie from truth a jail".*

Sam saw Mass Jim with a pair of rubber boots on his feet one day and he says to Miss Bertie, *"when you go back to town see if you can get one of these for me".* The next time Miss Bertie went to town she looked for the pair of boots for Sam. Miss Bertie could not find any size to fit Sam and when Miss Bertie come from town, Sam come for his boots. Aunt Bertie say "Sam the did not have your size." Sam said to Miss Bertie, *"Wha size Mass Jim wear"* Miss Bertie says, *"size eight".* Sam replied *"you could a buy two pairs then and me would a put them together and make one pair. Because Mass Jim wear eight and me wear sixteen so two eights would a make de sixteen".*

A young lady was going to town to buy a pair of shoes. So her mother told her to make sure that you ask for the proper shoes. Her mother told her that she needed size eight, color brown. The young girl asked the sale person for a pair of size brown color eight shoes. The sales person said we don't sell that. The girl went outside the store making up big noise saying *"Me come a town go buy me pair of shoes, me want size browns and colors eight and de man a tell me they no sell that"*. To top it all off it was only one pair of Bata Bus the girl was going to buy. (Bata Bus was a kind of plastic slipper they sold in those days).

There was a certain man name Mingo. If anyone bothered him, he had a reputation for always saying he was going to kill somebody or he would just do other mischief. There was a certain mansion in Davy Hill and one Saturday night it burn down next thing Mingo was admitted to the hospital with severe burns. He say he was passing the building and saw the fire and go put it out. According to the nurses, Mingo smelled of Gasoline. The mansion me burned down shortly after a man called Lucky Sam had chased down a man and stabbed him in the bottom and had killed another man called Willie Bull. Yes, Lucky Sam was the last man to be hanged in Montserrat April 6, 1960. These two incidents warranted their own song and it went something like this;

An a how come, and a how come
and How com Mingo burn Mass Ted mansion
Man a stab na shoulder, man a stab na bottom
And all a dat a dun right here na St. John.

Many people say that Mingo killed himself. Mingo's brother had a rum shop in St. John's and he wanted to get even with this gentleman so one day he went to his brother's shop and put poison in a bottle of rum specifically for this man whom he knew was going to come into the shop. Unfortunately for Mingo, his brother switched the bottle and when Mingo came back to the shop later he poured himself a drink from the poisoned bottle. When the drink started burning his throat, he knew exactly what had happen. He said out loud, " *lord no more Mingo tonight Mingo gone.* Mingo did die that same night in the hospital. Whatever was in the bottle was so strong the doctors could not save him.

Now, you have to understand that while his was alive, people were afraid of Mingo because he was a "bad" man. He had about one acre of sweet potato planted when he died and nobody claimed it not his wife or his children. People just passed by and say that the potato were winking at them so people stop looking in the direction of the potato patch.   My sister Inez thought that people were just plain stupid in not digging up the potatoes and eating them because Mingo did not know he was going to die so he could not have done anything to the potatoes. So, Inez decide she was going to dig some potatoes and cook them and after the people saw that nothing happened to her, they decided to dig up the potatoes.

I remember hearing the story about this man calling his wedding off. You see this man was supposed to be getting married but he did not intend to go through with it. The wicked man let the father and mother of the bride prepare everything, they even killed the cattle for the after party. The ceremony was supposed to start at 2 p.m. At about 12 O'clock the man come up on the hill and shouted out to the girl's father *"Mass Dardy, Mass Dardy, the thing wey me me promise you, me nar doom again".* He was calling off the wedding and he never explained why.

I have this cousin everybody used to call Molly. Molly loved pretty panties. So, one day I washing my nice pink lacey panty that I got from America. I had just worn it the one time to church on Sunday and this was Monday. When I was going up to the shop I met Molly coming down the road and she said she was going to Ms. Brand. When I look back Molly disappeared. It dawned on me that she had to pass through my yard and I had left my pretty panty on the line so I hurry and put down the things I had in my hand and double back home. When I got back, no panty, no Molly. Later that evening I saw her up St Johns and she crying *"Wheezy me with child for you and you nar bother with me, but pickney whey no hear wha Marmy say drink pepper water, lime and salt"*. Anyway between all the crying I said to her *"Molly why you tek up me panty"*. She says to me, *"Ms. Irene if you have no panty and you want to beg me one, go ahead and beg but no tell nobody that me tek up you panty"*. The irony was she had the same panty on.

My cousin Molly had a lot of children, but no man would admit that he had relations with her. One thing I could tell you about Molly she did not tell lies about any man. If she called your name you were there. A lot of men got busted by Molly when they visit her at night and then pass her the next day and did not speak. The first time I ever had to go to court was when she called out a certain man name. The man was always walking with his head held high and pretending that he was too good for the likes of Molly, so she called him out. The gentleman was so upset that he punched Molly and knocked her down. My father James Allen was Molly's cousin and so he took Molly to the Police to press charges and I had to testify.

The gentleman in question was an acolyte in the church and everyone in St John's knew that she was pregnant for him but he was playing big and mighty and he didn't want Molly to call his name. Molly went into labor the same day of the court hearing and Molly wanted to have a boy so she could name him after his father, but she had a girl instead, so, she put an E before the boy name and named her baby after her father.

There was a prominent family in the north. The man was down to earth, but the wife and the daughters were down right prêt up and accordingly they turned their noses up at people and barely waned to say hello to anyone. School children say the man had an intimate encounter with Molly. The next morning one of the daughters were walking up the street and met Molly and passed by without saying hello. Molly said to her, *"What a way you a pass your good step mother and no say good morning, after your father and I had such a good thing going last night".*

When I heard that Molly was getting married we were all down in St John's clinic. I said to Molly, *" I hear you getting married I think I better start ordering my dress".* Molly replied, *"me nar go invite all like you so to me wedding, only big shots coming".* I was not invited, but like everyone else I went to watch the wedding. When Molly saw me in the road she step out and say *"Hi cousin I am Mrs. Foster".* A couple weeks after the grand wedding I met Molly stepping in Town I said to her *"Mrs. Foster where you going".* She looked at me and replied, *"a right up a court house me a go, to reverse Foster".*

There was this man who could not drink his tea unless it's boiling hot. He was sailing on a ship. When he got his tea, he complained that it was not hot enough. The cook put the tea can on the fire, and really made it hot. The mister put the can straight to his mouth and when the tea burn his throat and his lip. He open his mouth wide and say" *Lard, this is a big ship".*

This gentleman used to love to say. *"Me buy me dog for shilling, me call me dog bully. Me feed me dog bully till he backside get big and broad. Now me no like me dog bully".*

Everybody out North know about Trowdong: What a character. Every Monday morning, Trowdong in the Court House at Cudjoe head for swearing. The Magistrate said, *"why you here again before me Mr. Fenton".* Trowdong say, *"how would you like to park you car and somebody come and hit you car. Just come dung and hit you car for no reason".* The Magistrate replied, *" I would not like that at all".* Trowdong said *"well* that it is what happen to me why me a behave so bad and a say so much bad words. Me park me car right outside the court house, and de man come dong and hit me". The Magistrate left the bench, and went outside to see the car. He asked Trowdong to show him where the car was and Trowdong pointed to his donkey. The magistrate just shake his head and tell the baliff to get this crazy man out of his court.

On another occasion Trowdong went to court, and he realized the magistrate was going to send him to jail for swearing. He asked the magistrate, "Mr. Besson you come from Grenada, where you ......tek you toe nail and cut Rice bag and a who you a talk to". I cannot repeat here all the curse words that followed that rendition. The Magistrate sent him to jail anyway. He cursed all the way to his cell.

Trowdong was in Town one Wednesday drunk and he laid down and fell asleep. So when he woke up, all buses going to the North was gone. He decided the only way to get shelter, is to get arrested. So he started swearing. There were some rookie Policemen just fresh from training school and they did not know about Trowdong. All seasoned Police Officers would have left him alone. Anyway they arrested Trowdong. They put him in the cell and Trowdong started calling for his meal and his lawyer and every right that he had. He made such a ruckus that Mr. Bisset came and said to get him out of here. Bail him out. Throwdung realized he was in the same position. So he started asking for his money that was taken from him. He said, " me had me whatsee whatsee twenty five dollars in me pocket and these whatsy whatsy Police take me money from me" and he started naming names. He called one Inspector by name and claimed that he had taken twenty five dollars from him. Mr. Bissett gave him the twenty five dollars to get rid of him. Trowdung knew that it would take exactly twenty five dollars to get home by taxi

The other court room character was Johnny Mac Brown. Every Christmas Johnny Mac Brown tried to get arrested because he say when he in jail he bound to get his ham and turkey but he not sure if he will get any when he is out. If by Christmas Eve he didn't get arrested he got drunk and started darting across cars in the street. Of course he got arrested.

The very first time he was unhappy to be arrested is when the queen was coming to Montserrat. The police arrested all the crazy people so they would not disturb the Queen. Johnny was hopping mad.

One time Johnny got arrested for stealing six limes from Rankin's lime field. On the day of the trial Johnny pleaded not guilty. The Police was surprised as they caught Johnny red handed. The Police presented their side of the case, and then it was Johnny's turn. Johnny said, *"the Police tamper with the evidence, the first time they presented the limes, there were six green limes, today they come in with six yellow limes, these are not the same limes they arrested and charged me for"*. The magistrate dismissed the case. While the limes were in the custody of the Police they turned yellow. Go Johnny Mack.

There was this man that everyone used to call Cuttay. School children used to pick on him because he used to walk and talk to himself. There was a certain policeman who used to stand up for him so anytime anyone bothered him he used to run to the policeman house to complain. Anyway, this policeman went to America and he sent Cuttay some shirts and Cuttay sent back the message, *"way de pants dem"*. Another time the policeman sent some money to a lady friend of his to give to Cuttay and I went home for Christmas and ran into Cuttay and I asked him if he got the money he hurriedly walked away from me saying as he was going *"she no gee me none, she no gee me non"*, Cuttay thought I was going to ask back for the money, I guess he had more sense that anyone thought.

These two men say as teenage boys they started playing man. So they used to leave St John's and go to Baker Hill to pick up women. One night they were coming down Tang Canes River, they heard a noise coming down the road. One man was blind so he could not see. The other one say *"Lord a one funeral procession a come"*. It seems that the Jumbies were having a funeral procession and they inadvertently interrupted it. The blind man said that his head swelled big like a barrel and the hair was standing up on his head. The one who could see held on to the one who couldn't see because he was ready to fly down the river out of fright.

One night this gentleman was driving from St John's to town. When he reached Runaway Ghaut, he saw a small child standing in the road. He thought to himself, " *a wha dis small Pickney a do out ya"*. So he stopped his car and picked up the child and put him in the back seat. He started back on his way and he noticed that the child was standing in the back of the car and holding on to the top of the seat with a smile on his face. The man noticed that the child had a mouth full of teeth. The man said to the child, *"you so small and how you mouth so full of teethe"*. The child said to him *"suppose me tek off me clothes and let you see dong day"*.

One night this man was walking home, and it started to drizzle. The man sped up his walking, so he could get home before the pouring rain start. He ran inside his house and closed the door. The man said out loud *"I just escaped the rain"*. The Jumbie who was following him all the time said, *"I just escaped it too"*.

Have you ever seen the old people open a new bottle of rum or wine? They had to throw some on the ground for what they call friends and family. One learned lady that you think would have good sense used to call every dead name while she was dropping the drink on the ground. By the time she finished give the dead their drink nothing much would be left in the bottle. So she would open a new one and start the ceremony over again. I used to be frightened because I was not sure if the dead was really drinking.

Have you ever done something wrong and your siblings get punish for it and your parents swear that they are right. Well let me tell a story. Never believe all that you think you know about your children. One time I was going to mountain with Aunt Kate. That's my mother. She was eating a Yellow thing. Cutting it with a knife and eat it. After a while she say Irene you want a piece. I say no me no eat that. I was eating my mangoes and was very satisfied with that. However the next morning she tell me make sure I clean her room and make her bed before I leave for school for she have somebody, coming to look at the roof. I went in to clean the room and I saw the yellow thing wrapped in a wax paper in her room. I pinch off a piece to taste it and it tasted really good. So I work is so I pinch the yellow thing. When I was ready to go to school I went to pinch another piece but there was nothing to pinch, so I took up wax paper and all and throw in my bosom and off to school I went. When I got up by the gate I took out the paper and dropped it. When lunch time to come home from school I lagged back because I knew there was going to be trouble in paradise. As I reached the head of the pitch, I hear ruption down Collins Ghaut. Aunt Kate beating Mildred and Stanley for she cheese. When she beat them she say *"you all can't pin this one on Irene for she no eat cheese, yesterday I was giving her some and she refused it"*. I reached the house with water running down me eye. Seeing my poor brother and sister getting kill for something they did not do. Aunt Kate say come Irene no cry for the two thief I know it's not you. I was not crying for them I was crying for myself because I knew that they did not steal the cheese.

My grandmother had a buffet that she used to store food. There was all kinds of things inside that place. Ripe bananas, ripe mango. Sugar, bread and all the goodies that a grandmother could have. The one thing she did was to keep her key around her waist. Mass Wellington figure out a way to get in the buffet; he could take the door off the hinges, take out what he wanted from the back and put it back. Poor Barba while she was taking things from the front others were taking from the back so when she reached the middle nothing is back there.

You know how people could make a name stick to your family. My grandfather William Weekes was a very tall man so they call him a Bagger and so we are the Baggers.

They say this lady gave this man a pig to raise and he killed the pig and he never gave the woman any of it. Some time after the woman asked him for her pig and he say *"ants done eat it off"*. So they call him Ants and all his children surname ants.

There was my cousin John Knobs. Mass John was on his way back to mountain one evening. He say he lost his pipe and could not do without it. When he was nearly in mountain he met up with Aunt Molly she asked him, *"where you going cousin John'*. He say, *"me a go look for me pipe"*. He continued complaining that he had lost his pipe and was on his way back to look for it because a man could not do without his pipe all night. Aunt Molly said *"Mass John, the pipe is in your mouth"*.

The old people say that at one time somebody was stealing all the people food that they planted in far mountain, cutting their Bananas and things. So they decide to set up a trap. When they went in they caught a certain man stealing. When the men got to Cat Ghaut Hill. They called out to Missy Ogarro that they had caught the thief. Missy said, *Praise God, a who e be a?"* The men replied, *"Poppy dumbbell"*. Missy Ogarro was flabbergasted because he was her family. She replied "Ok God!"

This good lady went to Mr. Hampsey store to shop. She wanted to buy some ice cream. She picked up her shopping and went home and ate one of her Ice cream bars. When she was finished she said, *"Mr. Hampsey get a different brand of Ice cream, it taste good but it too greasy"*. It was a stick of butter the woman ate and thought was ice cream.

You remember when white people started coming to Montserrat and the girls get job to work in the homes. Well the white woman put out a head of lettuce, her bread and ham, and asked the young lady to prepare lunch. The young girl fried the lettuce and the ham and put it on the table for the people to eat.

There was a man name Elick, he used to go to church and he also loved to walk and talk and praise his God. One morning in the early fifties, he got up and said London calling. Every body thought he was nuts and started to call him London. Soon after, people started going to London. He had prophesied that London was calling.

I remember there were upper mission and lower mission in church. There was a certain parson who was preaching at lower mission, school children say he was having a relationship with one of the sisters. When he was ready for her he would say, *"sister can I use you"?* and she would reply *"brother how can I refuse you."*

There was a man who attended the Catholic Church but in the old days when it was communion time the parishioners only got the bread and the Priest drank the wine. The man was so vexed that when the priest started chanting in Latin and whatever the Priest would say he would repeat, *"Parson a drink off all the wine and no ge a we none"*, and the Priest would chant again and the man would say, *"Yes father, we all knows it".*

There was a certain Politician from out North who was sent to Guyana to represent Montserrat. He got up to speak at his first engagement. He said, *"Mr. High commission, Mr. Prime Minister, Ladies and Gentlemen"*, everyone was alert listening and the man continued, *"I have nothing to say".* He went to the next engagement and the people that were traveling with him said, *"you can't do that you have to speak up".* He promised that when he got to the other ceremony he would do better. He got up and said, *"welcome to all here, I forgot my papers"*, and sat down.

There was a man call Book, who did not have all his faculties about him. The one thing he was afraid of the most, was a doll. He see a doll and he would run. Book used to eat off his sister's bread and sugar. So, his sister decided that when she bought her bread and sugar, she was going to lock them in her trunk and put a doll on top of the trunk to keep out Book. When Book entered the house and saw the doll on top of the trunk, he started crying. Book picked up a big piece of stick, shut his eyes and hit the doll one blow and knocked it off the truck and got his bread and sugar.

Montserrat people used to give their children all kinds of names and when you get you birth Certificate, you find out that your name was different from what you thought. Martha Farrell was my godmother, and she used to tell me that during my christening Father Bevrin said name this child one of the Godparents gave you a name. I went to school as Irene Rupertha Allen. When I grew up and was about to take my first trip, I went to get my birth certificate. The registrar searched and could not find my name. they found my parents names and a baby girl that was born the same day that I was so they figured that it was me. When I looked at the birthday certificate I was in tears I ran in to my father and I gave him by birth certificate he looked at it and said *"girl I did not know that your mother was a jackass"*. My name was not Irene Allen at all. It was Sarah Ruputer Weekes. The story goes that Teacher Kitty gave me the name Rupertha and that they sent my brother Wellington to register me, but the register could not spell. My poor brother Wellington could not spell Rupertha either , so he wrote Ruputer. The story goes that a jumbie named Irene Osborne had come for my name after I was registered and everyone called me Irene after the dead woman and the name stuck.

There were two brothers John and Jimmy. John was doing very well and playing rich and big but Jimmy was poor. One day Jimmy went to John and said to him, *"John gee me sudden day, me poor"*. John say, *"who poor fart"*. Time went on and things started getting better for Jimmy, while John went broke. After a while John come to Jimmy and say, *"Jimmy help me out me broke"*. Jimmy say *"who broke piss"*.

The Anglican Church is very proud of their Mothers Union. They used to meet on Thursday evenings and have their meetings and then they use to plan their rallies all the women were dressed in their glory white dress and their hat. But leave it to the school children to come up with a wonderful song about mothers union. They used to sing.

There was this lady called Miss Lucky. She knew everybody's business and was able to interpret every dream, so they call her the dreamer. Sometimes if you stump your toe and it takes a little while to heal, because you have to walk with no shoe and dust get into your toe and Miss Lucky see you with your soar foot she would get a dream that night about what was wrong with you. She would never tell you what was wrong but she would rub your foot and tie it up and low and behold it would heal.

This man never wear shoes on his foot no matter what. His daughter was getting married so they convinced him that he had to put on a pair of soft walker or sneakers if you will. The day of the wedding he dressed in his soft walker. When the reception was going on, somebody noticed, that he had no shoes on. it was tied around his neck. He started complaining that he took them off because they were keeping him back. Later when he was walking he stumped his toe until it was bleeding, he looked at the sneakers and said, *"if me no me tek you off a you would a get dat"*. (If I did not take you off, you would be the one getting hit).

There was also Mass Tooto. He never wore a pair of shoes until his wedding day. He was given a pair of sneakers to wear. As soon as he got home, he took them off and put them in his trunk. When questioned why he did that, he said "That is a piece of metal." To him the sneakers were like gold and he did not think he should were them.

This lady had a shop and one morning when she came to open the shop, she saw some black powder running right across the shop door. The woman ran for her life saying, "somebody a wok obeah on me". This is what happened. Remember how you used to buy the coffee roll in the brown paper, well the boys were gambling and they stopped at Miss Lucy Chris and bought a pack of coffee grounds to go home and make coffee. When they were passing by the ladies store they started arguing as to who should hold the coffee as they were drunk. They started fighting over the coffee and the paper ripped and spilled the coffee in the shop yard. The woman never stepped foot back in her shop, so her husband came and sold everything that was in the store and she shut it down.

There was a woman who was friendly with a married man. The man's wife decided that she was going to curse out the woman. So she went over to the woman's house and stood up in the road and started cursing. She said *"breadfruit tree let go me husband, breadfruit tree you a one slut and a whore and me a go beat the day lights out a you if you no let go me husband"*. The woman took the man's wife to court house for threatening her. The wife said to the magistrate, *"me no me a talk to she, and de breadfruit tree me me a talk"*. The magistrate said to her, *"do you eat breadfruit*, and she answered *"yes sir"*. The magistrate said to her, *"Well if you eat breadfruit, what has the breadfruit tree done to you"*, she said *"nothing sir"*. The magistrate told her, *"I am charging you 500 shillings, just for cursing the breadfruit tree like that"*.

They say this man and his wife used to go to mountain to work but the man was so snooty, he did not want anyone to see him with no bundle on his head. So every time they finished working, the wife had to pack the food to cook, the wood to cook it with and the vines for the pigs to eat and carry it on her head. This went on for some time. One day the woman got so mad, she come home and cooked for her and her children. She pealed the food and put it on him plate and set the table for him. When the husband came he washed his hands and sat down to eat his dinner. When he took off the towel to go eat, it was raw food on the plate.

There was this lady who was the mother mercy for St. John's Church but Lord she could drink her rum. Every Thursday morning she went with Parson from house to house and give communion. By the time she reach home she drunk like a coot. When she see anybody watching her as she staggered into her house she would look back and say, " *is de Lord me serving*".

This woman was in church singing with her book upside down. When somebody point out to her that her book was upside down she say, *"a foolishness you talking you see a because me left handed"*.

This man had bags of flour and he had a watch man. The watch man keep on saying who steal Mr. Daly's flour is a Bajan. They later found the flour in the Watchman's house. He was from Barbados.

I remember that one year there was an election and there was a field of candidates for the Northeren seat. As it happens, there was no electricity in St. Johns so this particular candidate would come out early and set up his a Dynomite Engine and light up the whole of St. Johns Street. He would give all the shopkeepers money to share drinks, all the adults drank their beer and rum and the school children received free sodas. His meetings were the most popular and well attended, they had a carnival atmosphere. There was this man named Joe Sky whom he tapped to be his campaign manager because he was a very boisterous fellow. The candidate sure thought he would win so an election night he brought one of the best bands to play at his victory party. After the votes were counted, he only received two votes, the one he gave himself and the one from his campaign manager.

There was another politician who was doing poorly because according to people even though he was a good man, he was not eloquent. The night before election he had a meeting and he said *"if ah you no want me tomorrow, when a you go dung a school to vote, X me out"*. Sure enough, went people went down to the school to cast their vote, they put an X next to his name believing that they were crossing him out and of course, he won the election by a landslide.

Back in school days, we used to call our teachers names behind their backs one of our favorite nicknames was for this teacher '"Ralph". He was very sort and skinny so we used to call him Squeezer and one day he came to class and said *"you can call me squeezer or you can call me Ralph but if you call me Squeezer Ralph you will pay the fine"*.

There was a girl named Missy and rumor had it she stole a fowl. So you know how school children can be cruel and mischievous. Every time they see Missy, they started chanting, *"who see fowl fly"* and someone would answer " *me see fowl fly"*.

There was a man who stole a chicken and he said it was a Mangoose who took it. So they made up this song about him.

Sly Mongoose, dog know you name.
Sly Mangoose, you no have no shame
Mangoose go in the Misus kitchen
Take up one of she big fat chicken
Put um in a he vest cut pocket,
Sly Mangoose.

Mothers union, Mothers union,
what a great society,
some a thief and some a tell lie
and some put poison a yellow fig.

Chapter 8
SUPERSTITIONS

T HERE IS the myth about cats, especially black cats. Some people walking and see a black cat at night turn back because its bad luck. So I cannot comprehend that anybody would see a black cat at night and pick up. I hear that's what happened to my Godfather Ricky.

Ricky was driving home one night, in his big truck, and when he came to Nine Turn Ghaut he saw a black cat, looking pretty and crying. He got out of his truck picked up the cat and took it home. He got ready for bed and went to sleep. The next thing he know the cat started crying. *"You better take me back where you got me from."* The story is Ricky had to leave his house that night and carry back the cat.

You ever hear how dogs growl at night. They say they growl one way when its a live person and they growl another way when they see the dead. And when they howl somebody was going to die.

If the Cock crow before midnight, somebody was going to die.

If you have full moon during Christmas it will be a terrible year. Plenty people a go dead and some tragedy will occur.

There was this nice lady, she was a seamstress. She started to feel sick. She did not go the doctor as she swore somebody work obeah on her. So she drank every kind of bush and rub with red lavender day and night to drive away jumbie. As time went on she became gravely ill it turned out the woman had cervical cancer. No such thing as jumbie, or obeah, but you could not get her to believe other wise. Anyway the poor lady died. The funeral service was held at St John's Anglican Church. The service over and Pastor outside standing up with the big cross turn up to the woman house because the people say the woman's spirit was up in the house and she refused to get in the coffin. It was close to six o'clock before her spirit laid in the coffin because all of her dead relatives lead her down from the house to the coffin. People were afraid to go to sleep that night and for a long time after.

This man died suddenly and word was that he was a real womanizer so him and his wife was not getting along too well. So the wife and his sister came with two, two pounds bags of rice to put in the coffin for him to count. Someone saw them before they were able to put the rice in the coffin. They started grabbing for the bags and the bags burst and the rice fell in the coffin. The wife said, "*better yet he could start counting right away*". The put the dead body on top of the rice and bury him. There is a saying that goes, '*if you believe the dead is going to be a bad dead and come back for other people you put either rice or sand in the coffin and he have to count all of it before he can leave his coffin and come after anyone*". Because when he misses he has to start all over again. So the moral of the story is they never stop counting and they never come

Remember when somebody died, how they use to pass the children over the coffin. They also wash the children skin with the same soap that they used to wash the dead. Everybody use to shut up their house when the dead pass. Women bow to the coffin and men take off their hats.

There is a story that say when somebody died and some-body they do not like come into the room they start to pulporise. They dig up a devil grass and get a plate and put the grass in and place on the dead person stomach and the dead calm down.

Did you ever wonder what happened to the slaves when they were no longer useful. This is the story: When the slaves were no longer useful, they were made to sit out under a tree so the master could keep track of when they die. The poor slaves were afraid to go to sleep because as soon as they shut their eyes Master would say that they were dead. The master already had the coffins made, and as soon as they fall asleep, he had them taken to Cars Bay. One time this slave fell asleep and before you know it he was in the coffin. He woke up and shout out. *"Massa me no dead yet"*. The master say, *"Haul he go long, Haul he go long Tek him dung a stinking Bay"*.

Chapter 9

FRUITS AND FOODS CHILDREN LOVED

God's blessings, we were hardly hungry and starving.

The old folks used to say that Mango was not happy because according to her *"she was tired bearing fruit to feed people hungry belly pickney dem"*. But guava say, *"you stand day me have to hurry up and bear so me could feed de people hungry belly Pinckney and dem"*. Nobody ever say what sour sop, sugar apple, gooseberry, sea grapes, custard apple mansiport, sabacka, strawberry and all the other fruits that we had to eat. I even forget some of the names of the wild berries that used to be in Barzey mountain, Sweeney's mountain and far mountain that were available to us.

Who remember mango season, how they wake you up between four and five o'clock to pick up mango. How important mango was back then . One thing I can tell you, we had plenty of mango tree down in Collins Ghaut, but no matter how early you get up the Osborne's were first. If you got up at five o'clock they already come and gone, four o'clock they already come and gone three o'clock they already come and gone. Montserratians no matter how poor never use to be hungry or can't find something to eat, unless they lazy.

There was a certain woman in Collins ghaut every body me fraid to pick up she mango. She used to dress in a long white frock with a stick in her hand waiting for the children. Some people used to swear that a the devil under her mango tree. So the mango stay under her tree.

I remember when we used to pick the mangoes, dig a hole and put some wire grass at the bottom and cover up the hole and leave for about one week. When you went back the mangoes were "quail and sweet". But you have to be careful because if anybody find your mango hole when you go back to look for you mangoes the hole is empty.

There was a woman who went out and picked up two bucket of mangoes and put in her house because they say hurricane was coming. The next morning they find her in she house dead. She ate off the two bucket of mango during the night and the mango killed her.

You remember after Christmas and January begin how times used to be hard, because most people spend off everything for Christmas but your parents and knew how to make ends meet. They have the salt pork well salted and dried. They also have pigeon peas. So it's a piece of pork and pigeon peas in the pot with whatever else they could find.

Your mother ever tell you go bring the pork and you foot start to tremble because while she was gone, the children and them already pull out the meat and only left the pork skin? Come on now don't pretend.

There was also banibis peas. That course rough peas. People use to be ashamed when they have to resort to cook Banibis peas. That thing was course but put a piece of pork fat in it and you forget the coarseness.

Some of us remember toluma. You cook it or you grate it to get to get the meal to make porridge for the babies. Lord when a child is fed on tuluma pop you could tell. They used to be big and fat and puffy. Anytime the people used to see one poory person they say *"Lord he need a good bowl of tuluma pop"*.

There was also the arrowroot. When you sick and they want you to get better. They give you a cup of arrowroot pop and they swear you not only get better you get your strength back.

You remember the red herring how you put it in the fire and roast it or you throw some rum on top and roast it. Most times you eat it with breadfruit, or bread, or cumba. You remember cumba. It is made from the cassava. You have the cassava bread and you have the cumba. People, who did not have a baking stone to bake the cassava bread, put it in the iron pot on the fire and make cumba. Sometimes you add a little coconut with that and it is delicious.

You remember pick potato and milk. Yes you boil the potatoes in the skin and it becomes pick potato. Many children had pick potato either for breakfast or lunch and if you were blessed you will get a little cow milk with that.

They used to make flour pop too. That thing used to stick to your side man.

They made musha pop too. And Turn musha sometimes with pigeon peas or long foot cabbage.

Yes man, those were the days and corn pop too.

Who remember potato duckena. Yes the one you wrap in either banana, or cheney bush and use the cheney string to tie de bush.

Yes your grandmother used to buy quarter pound Salt fish and feed a nation with it. Everybody get a little piece with some onion and oil.

One ounce of butter. Remember the salt butter. You put a little bit of that in a hot bread right out of the oven and you taste heaven.

The Calabash was the best dish to eat out of. All the children used to carve their name on the calabash. When you keep water in the calabash or the Toto you don't have need for ice because the water is very cool and nice when you drink it.

On Fridays, the shopkeepers used to bake cake to sell. The best cake was the one they baked in the sardine tin. Yes every thing we used had another purpose. The sardine and herring tin were also used for baking but the cake that was done in the sardine tin was special.

We used to look forward to August and September when hurricane was travelling. Friends and families use to gather together either at Barba Weekes House or later at Aunt Daisy. They cook, eat and sing all night. I still want to know what they used to put in the black coffee. That thing had a special taste.

Chapter 10
MAROONS.

THIS IS how a maroon work. If somebody wanted to build a house, they gather all their material and all the carpenters, mason and other workers in the village gather on a special day and put that house up.

The women come and prepare the food. They kill a goat or sheep and cook goat water, white rice and some times ground provision and they feed those men. There was always plenty of rum. So they work, a so they call for the rum. Sometimes some of them get so drunk they cannot perform, but there was also somebody else to take their place. By the end of the day that house is almost done.

There was maroon to clear land to plant cotton. There was also maroon to plant cotton. The women cook salt fish with cocoa tee for breakfast and goat water with white rice or breadfruit for lunch. And you pour the rum either in the tin cup or the calabash. So they drink and so they work. Sometimes by the end of the day men were falling down drunk.

Chapter 11
SONGS

REMEMBER THE penny concerts. You sing, somebody pay to take you down and then somebody pay a little bit more and put you back up and they take you down and put you back up until they run out of money. Maybe you will be able to complete your song or poetry, just maybe.

There were certain individuals that were known for certain songs. No matter what occasion, you can bet that they would sing their favorite song.

Royal telephone. Sister Berty used to sing that song every where she go and people use to think that she crazy but it was a real song.

Ho my comrades. Aunt Ellen song for Sunday School. She marched all the way from St. John's Church to Carrs Bay sing while waving a tree branch in the air. She sang it at every concert.

There's a stranger at the door. Miss Stranger used to sing that at every concert.

More about Jesus. Barba Hagga use to sing at every concert.

There are also these favorites;

1. Bam chick a lay, a chigga foot maga
   Me grandmother me send me for water
   Tell me lay me no trouble nobody
   Dam nigga man come feel up me lala

2. All day all night Miss Maryanne
   Down by the seaside sifting sand
   Even little children love Maryanne
   Down by the seaside sifting sand
   Maryanne Maryanne won't you marry me

3. When I die
   Don't bury me at all
   Pickle my bones with alcohol
   A bottle of rum at my head and my feet
   And tell all the girls that me die from rum

4. Massa Bailey me no dead yet
   Massa Bailey me no dead yet

Chapter 12
CONCLUSION

M R WALT Disney described what he called the carousal of progress.

Man began from humble beginnings and then progressed to greatness.

Lets' follow the carousal of progress for Montserrat.

The slave trade was rampart in Montserrat as in all of the other islands. Our generation, knows very little or nothing and have never been enslaved, but our fore parents were. My grandmother told me that her parents were born in slavery. I am not going to dwell on that part of our heritage because it is distasteful and painful to go back to that past. I want my readers to remember Montserrat as it were when we were having fun and lived free.

Montserratians earned their livelihood mostly from tilling the soil. We were fed from the product that came from their labors. They used their hoe and many a morning, very early you would see especially the men, walking with their hoe on their shoulders, or thrown across the backs of their Donkeys. The donkey was their from of transportation. Most were bare foot. We progressed from donkeys, to horses, to Mackabee buses. Those big wooden busses that chugged along from the North, South, East that transported people to and from the city. The driver stopped on the way to collect his fare and you better have it ready my dear. Now we have progressed. Most Montserrations have their own personal vehicles.

Their were times past when the dwellings were thatched roof houses with Dirt or Mud for flooring. People were quite content and satisfied with their lives. But progress came. From thatched roof (Woyler) to shingle, Galvanize and slate roofing if you please.

There was the outhouse and the kitchen was always separated from the house. Fire wood was used to cook. One can see the smoke bellowing and the sweet smell of the cooking coming from the kitchen. We used to look at the smoke on our way home from school to determine how far the cooking gone. If the smoke is what they call green. (Plenty smoke coming up) they just start the cooking. If the smoke is real low the pot nearly cook. My Aunt Ellen God rest her soul, use to fool us all the time because we would come with our mouths long according to her if the smoke is green. She used to put the pig food to cook to fool us. For nearly fifty years now, there is no more thatch houses and surely no more out houses. The people use to go cart water either from other houses or from the Government pipes. No more, we have progressed beyond that. Everybody have water a dem yard. (In their yard) That's progress.

Very few people are tilling the soil and planting food. They wait for the boat to come from Dominica to buy their produce. We have progressed. We are no longer walking without shoes on our feet. There are beautiful houses on Montserrat, Government Jobs and other Jobs in the private sector. We can now live by other means and the need to be toiling in the fields is not necessary.

God has blessed us with plenty. After hurricane Hugo struck in 1989, the people picked up and rebuilt. The

Volcano has caused many to flee but I know my fellow Montserratians and I believe some will soon return.

We own our own Bank of Montserrat. Who would have thought? I congratulate my school mate and friend Hensey Fenton, who came up with this brilliant idea. He has not been given enough praise and thanks. I do so now. But as the old saying goes, *'a prophet have no honor in their country'*.

Let us continue the progress, not looking backwards but forward. We can still repeat our jokes, and jumbie stories because we have the sense to know some are true but most are tales, and the Obeah is just plain fantasy.

King Reality, my little brother, wrote one of the best songs about Montserrat and it goes like this

If you search for it on the map
It is smaller than a dot.
But never mind the size, it is my little paradise.
Oh Montserrat Aliaguana
Place of my birth I'll love you forever.
So let us put our hands together
Slaving for this land
Let us hope to see our children
Walking hand in hand
Aiming in one direction
Striving to save our Nation
Let us pave the way for a new and brighter day.

The development of this country
Is our responsibility
Oh we Breadfruit and we Mangoes
All the happy faces
How I love you so

I thank the Lord above
For this Island that I love
When I die no matter where

Let my bones be buried here
In Emerald City
Island of beauty,
Place of my birth
I'll love you forever.
So let us put our hands together
Slaving for this land
Let us hope to see our children
Walking hand in hand.
Aiming in one direction
Striving to save our nation
Let us pave the way for a
New and brighter day.
So Let us put out hands together
Slaving for this land
Let work to see our
Children walking hand in hand
Aiming in one direction
Striving to save our nation
Let us pave the way for a
New and brighter day.

Good, better, best.   My mother taught me that and I said it at every concert. I used to be proud because I made no mistakes. *"Good, Better, Best. I will never rest until my good becomes better and my better best".* One Sunday afternoon I went up and proudly recited my poem and to my shock Ismay Mundo said, "that little girl no tired say the same thing". I was crushed. I cried all the way home, but my mother assured me to keep on saying my poem if it is only in my heart for one day she said your good will become better and your better best. Thank you mom for your inspiring words. I continued to say my poem in my heart and surely my good has become better and my better my best.